The Tiara Club

✦ AT RUBY MANSIONS ✦

The Tiara Club

Princess Charlotte *and the* Birthday Ball
Princess Katie *and the* Silver Pony
Princess Daisy *and the* Dazzling Dragon
Princess Alice *and the* Magical Mirror
Princess Sophia *and the* Sparkling Surprise
Princess Emily *and the* Substitute Fairy

———◆———

The Tiara Club at Silver Towers

Princess Charlotte *and the* Enchanted Rose
Princess Katie *and the* Mixed-up Potion
Princess Daisy *and the* Magical Merry-Go-Round
Princess Alice *and the* Glass Slipper
Princess Sophia *and the* Prince's Party
Princess Emily *and the* Wishing Star

———◆———

The Tiara Club at Ruby Mansions

Princess Chloe *and the* Primrose Petticoats
Princess Georgia *and the* Shimmering Pearl
Princess Olivia *and the* Velvet Cape
Princess Lauren *and the* Diamond Necklace
Princess Amy *and the* Forgetting Dust

~ VIVIAN FRENCH ~

The *Tiara* *Club*

✦ AT RUBY MANSIONS ✦

Princess Jessica
~ AND THE ~
Best-Friend Bracelet

KATHERINE TEGEN BOOKS
HarperTrophy®
An Imprint of HarperCollins Publishers

The Tiara Club at Ruby Mansions:
Princess Jessica and the Best-Friend Bracelet
Text copyright © 2008 by Vivian French
Illustrations copyright © 2008 by Orchard Books
All rights reserved. Printed in the United States of America.
A paperback edition of this book was published in the United
Kingdom in 2007 by Orchard Books.

Library of Congress Catalog Card Number: 2007905256
ISBN 978-0-06-143485-3

Typography by Amy Ryan
❖
First U.S. edition, 2008

For my very own Princess Jessica,
with MUCH love
x x x—V.F.

The Royal Palace Academy
for the Preparation of Perfect Princesses
(Known to our students as "The Princess Academy")

OUR SCHOOL MOTTO:
*A Perfect Princess always thinks of others before herself,
and is kind, caring, and truthful.*

**Ruby Mansions offers a complete education for
Tiara Club princesses with emphasis on the
creative arts. The curriculum includes:**

Innovative Ideas for our Friendship Festival

Designing Floral Bouquets (all thorns will be removed)

Ballet for Grace and Poise

*A visit to the Diamond Exhibition
(on the joyous occasion of Queen Fabiola's birthday)*

**Our principal, Queen Fabiola, is present at all times,
and students are in the excellent care of the head fairy
godmother, Fairy G., and her assistant, Fairy Angora.**

OUR RESIDENT STAFF & VISITING EXPERTS INCLUDE:

KING BERNARDO IV *(Ruby Mansions Governor)*

LADY ARAMINTA *(Princess Academy Matron)*

LADY HARRIS *(Secretary to Queen Fabiola)*

QUEEN MOTHER MATILDA *(Etiquette, Posture, and Flower Arranging)*

We award tiara points to encourage our
Tiara Club princesses toward the next level.
All princesses who earn enough points at Ruby
Mansions will attend a celebration ball, where they
will be presented with their Ruby Sashes.

Ruby Sash Tiara Club princesses are invited
to go on to Pearl Palace, our very special
residence for Perfect Princesses, where they may
continue their education at a higher level.

PLEASE NOTE:
Princesses are expected to arrive
at the Academy with a *minimum* of:

TWENTY BALL GOWNS
*(with all necessary hoops,
petticoats, etc.)*

TWELVE DAY-DRESSES

SEVEN GOWNS
*suitable for garden parties
and other special daytime
occasions*

TWELVE TIARAS

DANCING SHOES
five pairs

VELVET SLIPPERS
three pairs

RIDING BOOTS
two pairs

*Cloaks, muffs, stoles, gloves,
and other essential
accessories, as required*

Hi! It's me—Princess Jessica!

And it's lovely to meet you, and to know you're here at Ruby Mansions with me and my friends from the Poppy Room.

Have you met us all? There's Chloe, Olivia, Lauren, Georgia, Amy, and me.

And Charlotte, Katie, Daisy, Alice, Sophia, and Emily are in the Rose Room right next door to us. Things would be just about perfect if only those horrible twins, Diamonde and Gruella, weren't here. They get worse and worse—especially Diamonde!

"*I* just wish I knew where it was," Princess Amy said for about the twentieth time that morning, and Princess Chloe, Princess Olivia, and I nodded sympathetically.

We were sitting in the Home-work Room trying to finish our

math assignments, but Amy had lost her watch and we weren't really concentrating.

"Could you have left it in the coatroom?" Olivia asked.

Amy shook her head. "I've looked everywhere. It's completely disappeared."

I was about to suggest that Amy look in her pockets when Princess Lauren rushed in. "Have you heard?" she asked. "There's going to be a Festival of Friendship! Fairy G. told me. And there's a competition before that too. We've got to think of something special to do for our friends, and the room with the

best idea gets to ride at the head of
a Friendship Procession all the way
around the town."

"Ride?" Chloe sat up very straight. "You mean, actually riding on ponies?"

Lauren nodded and her eyes were sparkling. "Isn't it just fantastic? The stables are full of the sweetest little dapple gray ponies—oops!" Lauren clapped her hands over her mouth.

"Fairy G. told me not to tell! It's supposed to be a surprise. Oh, we absolutely have to win! Hurry up, and then we can make our plans."

And she dashed off.

We looked at one another. "It does sound amazing," I said. "Dapple gray ponies! Won't they be cute?"

"And we ought to win, because we Poppy Roomers are the best friends ever," Olivia added.

Chloe nibbled the end of her pencil. "I hope the ponies aren't too frisky. Just imagine falling off in front of a whole crowd of people! Wouldn't it be embarrassing?"

"You'll be okay," I said. "Riding's easy."

Amy looked at me. "Actually," she said, "it isn't easy if you're scared." She bit her lip. "Can I tell you a secret? I fell off a pony when I was little, and I've been terrified of riding ever since. I still have nightmares about it. It was horrible!"

"Didn't they make you get right back on?" I asked. "They made me."

Amy turned very pink. "My mother wouldn't let me," she said. "And please don't tell anyone else! Please. If we win, I'm going to try really hard to be brave . . ."

Of course we all promised. Perfect Princesses *never* tell one another's secrets.

"Actually, Fairy G. would never make you ride unless you wanted to," Chloe said. (Fairy G. is our Fairy Godmother, and she takes care of us.) "And we may not win anyway. Let's get this homework finished, and then we can meet up with Princess Lauren and Princess Georgia and think of some ideas."

"And ask them if they've found my watch," Amy said. "Although I don't think I'll ever see it again."

I looked at my math book and groaned. "How on earth are we supposed to know how much it costs to clean the palace windows?"

"What about answering the

question with, 'It depends how many windows there are'?" Olivia suggested.

"I think that's really smart," I said.

The others agreed, and we put our notebooks into our lockers and hurried off. I was last, and it was only as I was about to go through the door that I noticed the twins. They were lurking in the corner of the Homework Room, almost hidden behind a bookcase. They

were whispering together and looking pleased with themselves. I
couldn't help thinking they'd been
spying on us, but I told myself, *A
Perfect Princess always thinks the
best of others.* I ran after my
friends—and tripped over a rug as I
reached the hallway.

Wham!

It took my breath away, and I felt so silly. I picked myself up as quickly as I could, and that's when I saw Amy's watch lying in a corner. I let out a whoop of joy—Amy would be so happy to see it again! I put it in my pocket, dusted myself off, and left.

Chapter Two

When I came hurrying into the Recreation Room, Princess Georgia was smoothing out a piece of paper, Chloe was clutching a pencil, and Lauren was leaning over her shoulder.

"Where's Amy?" I asked as I joined them.

"She's gone with Olivia to check the bulletin board for the competition rules," Lauren explained.

"Here's Olivia now." Lauren

waved as Olivia came puffing up and flung herself onto the sofa.

"We've got to think of 'Creative Ways to Make a Friend Feel Special,'" Olivia said. "And we don't just get to ride at the front of the procession if we win—we also get ten tiara points each!"

I was beginning to wonder if Amy had gone to look for her watch upstairs. I was dying to see her face when I handed it over!

"Is Amy going to be long?" I asked.

Olivia shrugged. "I left her by the bulletin board," she said. "She was talking to Princess Diamonde and Princess Gruella—"

"I'll go and find her," I said. "I've got a surprise for her!" And I jumped up and rushed off.

I ran down the hall, and I was lucky I didn't meet any teachers— they'd have given me a million minus tiara points for running. I could see Diamonde, Gruella, and Amy by the bulletin board, and I bounced up to them.

"Guess what?" I said to Amy. "Look what I found!" And I held out her watch.

"Thank you!" Amy said. She took it and waved it at Diamonde. "Isn't it wonderful to have friends who take care of you?"

Diamonde turned toward me, and I saw her wink at Gruella.

"Yes," she said, and she looked really nasty. "It's wonderful to have friends—if they really *are* friends. But you see, Amy, we've got something we feel we ought to tell you about Princess Jessica." And she shook her head as if she was very upset. "Isn't that right, Gruella?"

Gruella nodded. "That's right, Diamonde."

"Amy," Diamonde went on, "I'm afraid Jessica told us your secret. She told us you're a poor little scaredy-cat—and you're really scared of riding!"

I was so taken by surprise I couldn't say a word. I just

stared at Diamonde.

And then the most dreadful
thing happened. Amy looked at me
and her eyes filled with tears.

"How *could* you?" she asked. "I didn't think you'd ever do something like that. I really, really didn't!" She let out a little sob and ran away down the hall.

Diamonde smiled triumphantly.

"And we thought you were such special friends," she said. "Oh, dear!" And then she and Gruella marched off in the other direction, sniggering.

I was so angry, and really upset as well. How could Amy think I'd do something so horrible? She was my friend. I'd never tell any of her secrets. I took a deep breath and walked slowly back to the Recreation Room.

As soon as I got through the door, I knew they'd been talking about what had happened. Amy was sitting on a sofa, and Lauren and Georgia had their arms around her. As I came over to them, Amy sniffed and buried her nose in her hankie. Chloe glared at me.

"Honestly, Jessica," she said. "How could you be so mean? Amy said you told the twins about how she's scared of riding—and you

promised you wouldn't tell!"

"But I didn't!" I protested. "Really I didn't!"

Olivia shook her head. "I'm sorry, Jess," she said. "It must have been you. How else could they have known? Amy only told us ten

minutes ago in the Homework Room."

I had a sudden flash of inspiration.

"But the twins were there too! I saw them as I was leaving—they must have overheard us talking! They were behind the bookcase." Even as I explained, my voice died away. I could see from my friends' faces they didn't believe me.

Chloe frowned. "*I* didn't see them there." She turned to Olivia. "Did you?"

Olivia shook her head. "No," she said.

Amy gave me a sad look. "I'm

sure you didn't mean to tell," she said. "I suspect it just sort of slipped out, and then the twins made the most of it."

I began to feel sick. Ever since I'd been at the Princess Academy I'd been best friends with everyone in the Poppy Room, and now Lauren was looking at me as if I was as nasty as Diamonde!

Amy blew her nose hard. "Let's

try and forget about it," she said bravely. "If I wasn't so nervous about riding, it would never have happened. Let's think about what we're going to do for the competition."

"You're a Perfect Princess," Chloe said, and she gave Amy a

hug. "You really, truly are!"

"That's right." Olivia gave me a frosty look. "And I think Jessica should say she's sorry."

"But I haven't *done* anything!" I said. Then I couldn't help it. I burst into tears and ran out of the room. No one ran after me, and I knew why. They thought I was crying because I was guilty—but I wasn't. I was crying because they didn't believe me.

Chapter Three

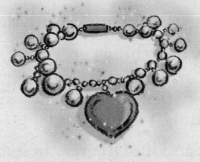

I rushed to the bathroom so nobody would see me, but when I got there Emily was washing her hands.

"Are you okay?" she asked.

I swallowed and nodded. "I'm fine," I said, and I blew my nose

hard. Emily looked at me doubt-
fully.

"Are you sure?" she asked.

"Yes, thank you." And I almost
was. When things go wrong, I like
to do things, and I'd thought of
something I could do. I'd go to the
library and find the very best idea for
the Friendship Festival competition.
A part of me was thinking, *That'll
show them!*

I was about to march out of the
bathroom when Emily called me
back. "I'm so sorry," she said, "but
could you tie up my bracelet for
me?"

"Of course," I said, and I took

the bracelet from her. "Oh! Isn't it pretty?"

Emily smiled. "It's a friendship bracelet," she said. "Daisy made it for me over vacation, and I always wear it."

I nearly hugged her. Friendship bracelets! Wouldn't that be the best idea ever? But then I wondered if Emily had thought of it for the Rose Room.

"No," she said when I asked her. "We're going to suggest making feathery fans. Don't say I told you!"

"I won't," I promised, and as I hurried away I felt so much better. I was about to head back to the Recreation Room when I had another idea: Why don't I see if I could make a bracelet all by myself? And then I could show the others!

I practically skipped up to the Craft Room, and I was in luck. The door was open, and Fairy Angora (she's our assistant Fairy Godmother) was cleaning up. She looked a bit surprised to see me, but all she said was, "Can I help you, my darling?"

"Yes, please!" I said. "I want to make a friendship bracelet."

Fairy Angora smiled. "Now that's a wonderful idea!"

"I know," I said. "But I want to try one out first."

The next hour or so whizzed by. Fairy Angora showed me where things were, and I made the cutest friendship bracelet! It had pink

twinkly beads and tiny pink hearts, and a little silver clasp shaped like two hands holding each other.

"Thank you very much," I said when it was finished.

"Aren't you going to wear it?" Fairy Angora asked.

I hesitated. "I don't think so," I said. Somehow it felt as if it might be bad luck to wear the bracelet before I'd fixed things with my friends.

Fairy Angora smiled at me. "I see. Good luck!"

For a moment I wondered if she knew what had happened between Amy and me, but she couldn't have. All the same, it felt a little strange.

The bedtime bell rang while I was walking back, so I quickly made my way up to the Poppy Room.

Do you know what it's like when you come into a room and everybody suddenly stops talking, and you just know they were talking about you? Well, that's what happened to me.

Chloe said, "We've been deciding what we're going to suggest for the competition. We thought our idea could be to make pretty little cushions, and they'll be exactly the right size to put tiaras on! What do you think?"

"I was thinking of friendship bracelets," I said, and I held mine out.

"Oooh!" Georgia's eyes lit up, and I saw Olivia smile, but Chloe shifted from foot to foot as if she was embarrassed.

"Um . . . I thought we'd sort of decided on the little cushions," she said.

"That's right." Lauren folded her arms. "It was Amy's idea, and we thought it might cheer her up if we chose it." She gave me a meaningful look. "She's still really upset."

The sick feeling in my stomach suddenly got worse. "Oh," I said. And I put my bracelet away in my pocket.

I didn't sleep well that night. It was so strange. I absolutely knew I hadn't told the twins about Amy being scared of riding, but I still felt as if I'd done something terrible.

"But I haven't," I told myself firmly. "I really, really haven't. . . ."

At last I drifted off to sleep, and I had all kinds of weird dreams.

And then the alarm went off and it was time to get up.

Chapter Four

The day didn't start well. No one talked to me at breakfast. When I walked into the dining hall, I found there wasn't a seat for me at our usual table. I had to go and sit by myself.

Diamonde and Gruella looked

at me and immediately started giggling. "Look!" Diamonde sneered. "What's happened to the Poppy Roomers?"

Gruella tilted her head to one side. "I wonder why nobody's talking to Jessica? Aren't the Poppy

Roomers supposed to be the best friends ever?"

"That's right." Diamonde snorted. "So they're *bound* to get to ride at the head of the Friendship Procession. . . ."

"And then poor Amy will fall off

her dear little pony!" Gruella just about fell off her chair, she was laughing so much.

I didn't know what to do. I stared at the table in front of me and did my best to ignore them. The very next moment the door burst open, and Fairy G. came bounding into the room.

"Now, my dears," she boomed. "Time for the competition to see which dormitory has the best idea for 'Creative Ways to Make a Friend Feel Special'! Lily Room, what have you thought of?"

Princess Hannah stood up. "We've thought of embroidering

hankies," she said, "with little tiaras
in each corner."

Fairy G. said, "Fine! Fine! And
what about the Tulip Room?"

The Tulip Room said their idea was to spend every Monday morning polishing their friends' tiaras, and the Sunflower Room wanted to arrange a special Friendship Tea Party. Then Gruella burst out, "You haven't asked us, Fairy G.!"

"That's right." Diamonde tossed back her hair. "We've got the best idea ever. We're going to give every princess in the school our autographs!"

"So when we're famous, they'll be able to frame them," Gruella added.

Fairy G. didn't look very impressed. She said, "I see. Now,

let's hear from the Rose Room."

Emily told her about making fans. Fairy G. nodded. "And what about the Poppy Room? Have you got a sparkling idea to make your friends feel really special?"

"*They* don't deserve to win, Fairy

G.," Diamonde interrupted rudely. "They're not even speaking to Jessica!"

"That's right," Gruella added. "*We* should be riding those dapple gray ponies, not them!"

Fairy G. gave Gruella the oddest

look. "Princess Gruella," she said, and something in her voice made us all sit up very straight and pay attention, "might I ask how you know what color the ponies are?"

"Lauren said they were dapple gray," Gruella smirked. "We both

heard her, didn't we, Diamonde? When we were in the Homework Room—*ow*!"

She stopped with a squeal. Diamonde had pinched her.

All my friends from the Poppy Room gasped and stared at me and began to talk all at once.

Fairy G. began to swell, which is what she always does when she's angry.

"Just what is the meaning of this?" she bellowed.

Amy stepped forward and sank into a deep curtsey. "Fairy G.," she said, and her voice was shaking, "I don't think any of us from the

Poppy Room deserve to ride in the Friendship Procession, except Jessica." She looked over at Lauren and the others. "We—we've just been the worst friends ever to poor Jess, and I want to tell her how very, very sorry I am." She walked over to me and took my hand. "Will you ever forgive me?"

I blushed bright red. "Of course," I mumbled.

"Poppy Room!" Fairy G.'s voice was so loud I jumped. "Kindly explain!"

Chloe put her hand up. "Fairy G.," she said, "Amy told us a secret, and we didn't know the twins were hiding in the Homework Room and overheard us. And then they told Amy it was Jessica who had told them."

Olivia nodded. "Jessica did say she'd seen them in the Homework

Room, but we didn't believe her—"

"But Jessica couldn't have seen us!" Gruella squealed. "We were hiding behind the bookcase!"

Fairy G. gave Gruella a piercing look. "And why was that, Gruella?" she asked.

Gruella hung her head and didn't answer.

"Diamonde? Can you tell me?" Fairy G. asked, but Diamonde

wouldn't say anything either. She stared hard at the table in front of her and picked at her fingernail.

Fairy G. folded her arms. "One of the most important things about being friends," she said, "is to be able to sort out misunderstandings

and say you're sorry. Jessica, what do you have to say?"

"All I have to say," I began, "is that I've got the best friends in all the world!"

"Excellent," Fairy G. said. "Now, what have you got to say, Diamonde and Gruella?"

There was a long silence and then the twins muttered, "Sorry."

"Now that's dealt with," Fairy G. said. She looked at Amy. "So, I never did get to hear what the Poppy Room's idea to make their friends feel special was?"

Amy, Chloe, Lauren, Olivia, and Georgia looked at one another, and

then at me. "Friendship bracelets!"
they said, all together.

"Very good," Fairy G. said. "A
splendid idea."

An idea popped into my head.

"Excuse me," I said, "but could we make bracelets for Diamonde and Gruella too?"

Fairy G. raised her eyebrows. "May I ask why?"

"Because they need to know how to be friends more than any of us," I said, and I could feel myself blushing all over again.

"Well said." Fairy G. smiled a huge beaming smile. "And for that answer, I declare the Poppy Room the winners! The Poppy Room will ride at the head of the Friendship Procession on dapple gray ponies!"

Chapter Five

*T*he Festival of Friendship was *wonderful.* By the time it arrived, I was so tired of my friends telling me how sorry they were, I had to tell them we wouldn't be friends if they ever mentioned it again!

And guess what? Fairy G. tapped

my bracelet with her wand and suddenly there were eight of them. One for each of us, and one each for Diamonde and Gruella—who did not say thank you.

Amy was fine. It turned out that Fairy G. was going to ride in the prettiest silver carriage with Fairy Angora, and they asked if Amy would be kind enough to keep

them company. We went around
and around the town, bowing and
smiling and waving until I thought
my arm would fall off!

And then in the evening there

was a huge picnic beside the Princess Academy Lake, with music and dancing. The trees were hung with sparkly lights, and Chinese lanterns shone over the tables piled high with the most delicious things to eat—and there were cute little pink satin cushions to sit on. We wore our most summery ball gowns, and we danced and danced until the sky was a deep velvety blue, and sprinkled with thousands of tiny silver stars.

But the best moment came as I was going up to the Poppy Room at the end of the day. Gruella was leaning against the wall outside the

door, and as I walked past she pushed something into my hand.

"Sorry," she mumbled, and then she was gone.

When I looked down, I found I was holding a little note. It said:

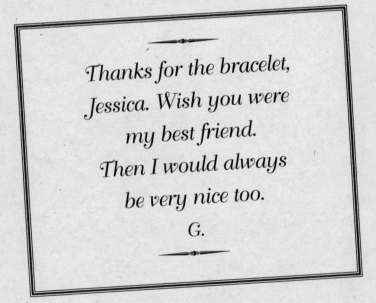

Thanks for the bracelet, Jessica. Wish you were my best friend. Then I would always be very nice too.

G.

And when I was lying in bed that night, I was so happy because I had so many wonderful friends—and I'm so glad you're my friend too!

What happens next?

FIND OUT IN
Princess Georgia
∾ AND THE ∾
Shimmering Pearl

Hello! I'm very pleased to meet you. I'm Princess Georgia. And Chloe, Jessica, Olivia, Lauren, and Amy share the Poppy Room with me—and we're very best friends. We're trying to be Perfect Princesses. But—guess what! It isn't always easy.

I'm so glad you're here at Ruby Mansions with us—but watch out for the horrible twins, Diamonde and Gruella.

They're so mean.

But we'll take care of you.

You're our friend!

8-12-15

You are cordially invited
to the Royal Princess Academy

Introducing the new class of princesses
at Ruby Mansions

All Tiara Club books have a secret word hidden in the illustrations. Can you find them? Go to www.tiaraclubbooks.com and enter the hidden words for more fun!

Katherine Tegen Books
An Imprint of HarperCollinsPublishers

HarperTrophy®
An Imprint of HarperCollinsPublishers